To Robin and Leo from your
proud mama bear—JEM

W

PENGUIN WORKSHOP
An imprint of Penguin Random House LLC, New York

First published in the United States of America by Penguin Workshop,
an imprint of Penguin Random House LLC, New York, 2024

Copyright © 2024 by Jennifer Morris

Visit us online at penguinrandomhouse.com.

Library of Congress Cataloging-in-Publication Data is available.

Manufactured in China

ISBN 9780593752029   10 9 8 7 6 5 4 3 2 1 TOPL

Design by Jay Emmanuel

Sharing Is UnBEARable!

by J. E. Morris

Penguin Workshop

One day, Orson went for a walk in the woods.
(Bears like to take walks.)

On his walk, he found a big rock.

Wow, that is a big rock!

The rock was smooth and warm from the sun. It was a good rock.

Ah, this is a good rock.

It was the perfect spot for Orson to take a nap. (Bears like to take naps.)

Yawn.

The very same day, Izzy took a walk, too.
(I told you, bears like to take walks.)

She also found a big rock.

Oh, that rock is a doozy!

Izzy's rock was warm and smooth, just like Orson's.

This is a good napping rock.

There was just one problem.

wiggle
wiggle

Orson and Izzy had found the SAME rock!

The rock was big enough for two.
But there was something I didn't tell you.

Izzy had an idea.

What if we took turns on the rock?

Took turns?

That sounds a lot like sharing.

Izzy took a nap on the rock.
She took a long, long, loooooooooooooong nap.

Orson was not happy.

He got a bucket of icy cold water.

The bears had reached a stalemate.

A stalemate is when no one will give in.
(Bears can be very stubborn.)

Then Orson had an idea.

I'll be right back.

He returned with something very heavy.

Grrrrrrr!

Izzy tried napping on the new rock.

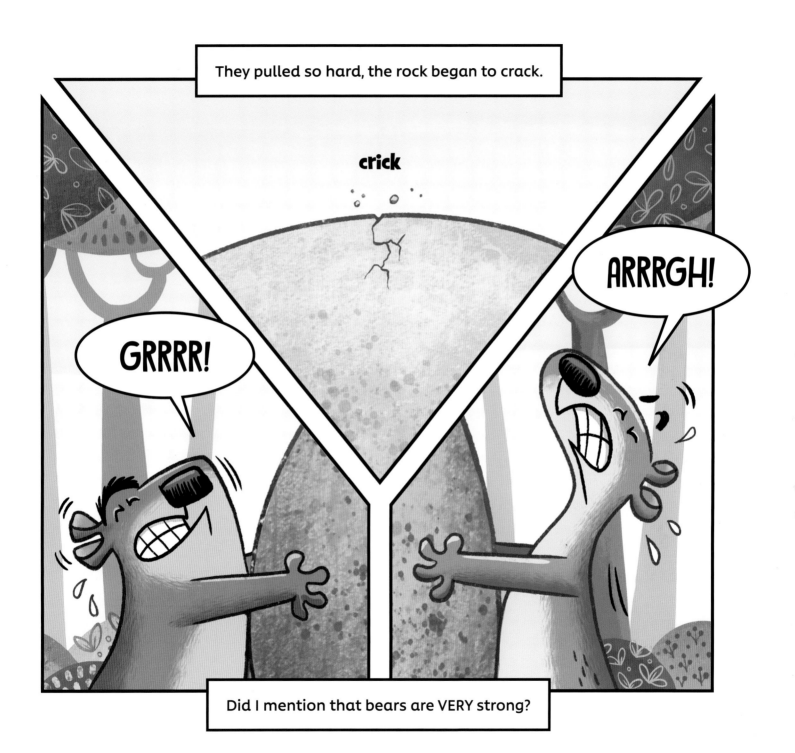

KErR

But Orson and Izzy kept fighting. (I told you bears are stubborn.)

Izzy and Orson sat on the cold, wet, muddy ground.

Orson and Izzy used the sticky mud to fix the rock.

A bird flew by and landed on the rock.

flap
flap

The bird wanted to take a nap on the big, smooth, warm rock.
(Did I tell you that birds like to take naps, too?)

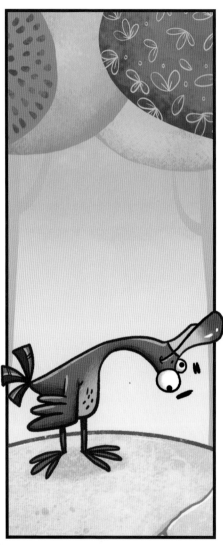

Orson and Izzy confronted the interloper.
(An interloper is someone who is not welcome.)

Izzy heard something.

Orson heard it, too.

Orson and Izzy asked the bird to join them on the rock.

Hey, bird, do you want to join us?

Orson, Izzy, and the bird took a nap on the big rock together.

I guess I was wrong.

Bears CAN share, after all.